1/27

Oh No, Domino!

To Jackie—
oh yes,
READ!

— WITH LOVE!

Adlerman books
• • • • • • • • • •

Africa Calling, Nighttime Falling
Rock-a-bye Baby
Songs for America's Children
How Much Wood Could a Woodchuck Chuck?
Oh No, Domino!

by Kin Eagle (Danny and Kim's pen name)
(illustrated by Roby Gilbert)
• • • • • • • • • •

It's Raining, It's Pouring
Hey, Diddle Diddle
Rub a Dub Dub
Humpty Dumpty

Adlerman music
• • • • • • • • • •

One Size Fits All
Listen UP!

Oh No, Domino!

by Kim ADlerman

Music by Danny ADlerman

with reading by Kevin Kammeraad

● ● ● ● ● ●

The Kids at Our House

Oh no, Maxx. This book's for you!
—With love

Text and illustrations copyright © 2007 by Kim Adlerman
Lyrics and music copyright © 2007 by Danny Adlerman

The Kids at Our House
47 Stoneham Place
Metuchen, NJ 08840

www.dannyandkim.com
info@dannyandkim.com

Library of Congress Cataloging-in-Publication Data available on request

ISBN-10: 0-9705773-7-0 (hc)   ISBN-13: 978-09705773-7-5 (hc)
ISBN-10: 0-9705773-8-9 (sc)   ISBN-13: 978-09705773-8-2 (sc)

10 9 8 7 6 5 4 3 2 1 (hc)   10 9 8 7 6 5 4 3 2 1 (sc)

The display type was set in Billy Bold.
The text type was set in Humanist 521 Bold.
Manufactured in China.
Book production and design by *The Kids at Our House*

Danny and Kim make school and library appearances. In fact, we appear in front of big people, too—at conferences, county reading councils, professional development workshops…we can fit into most any venue you can think of! For more information, as well as free activities and activity guides, check out www.dannyandkim.com.

"Domino! Let's play ball!

Ana, cats can't catch.
Sorry, dogs only."

"Go, Domino!"

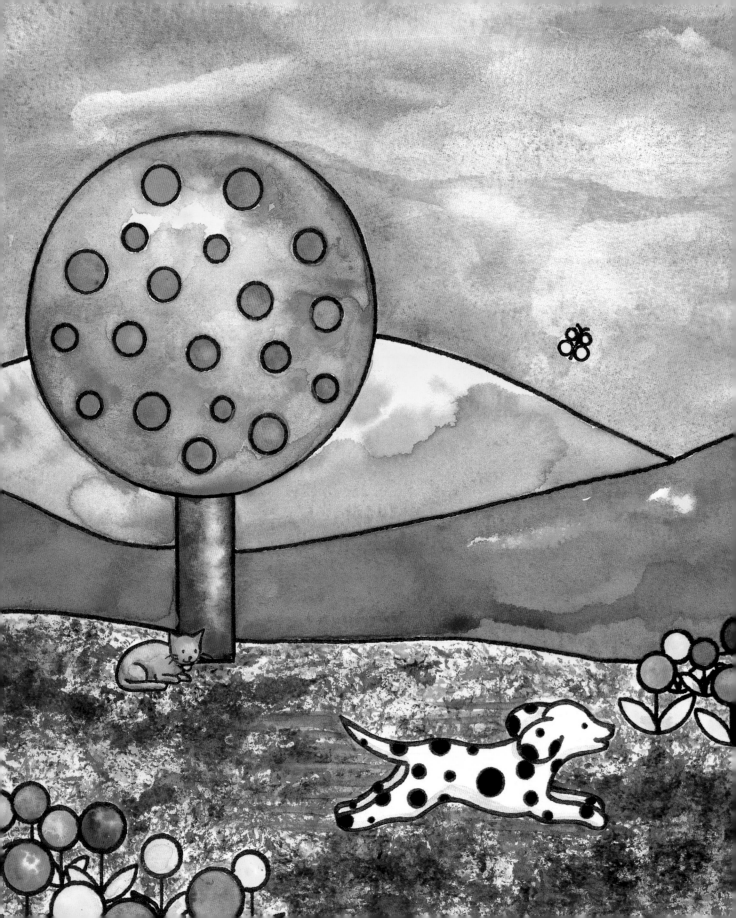

"Oh no, Domino.
That's not the ball. That's a flower.
Get the *ball*, Domino!"

"Oh no, Domino.
That's not the ball. That's an apple.
Get the *ball*, Domino!"

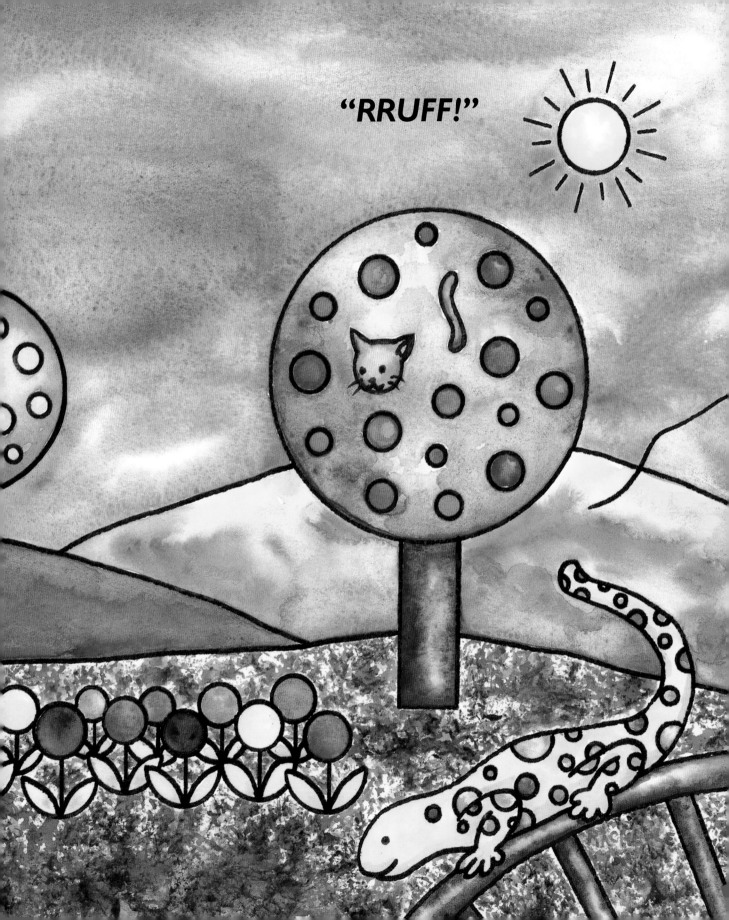

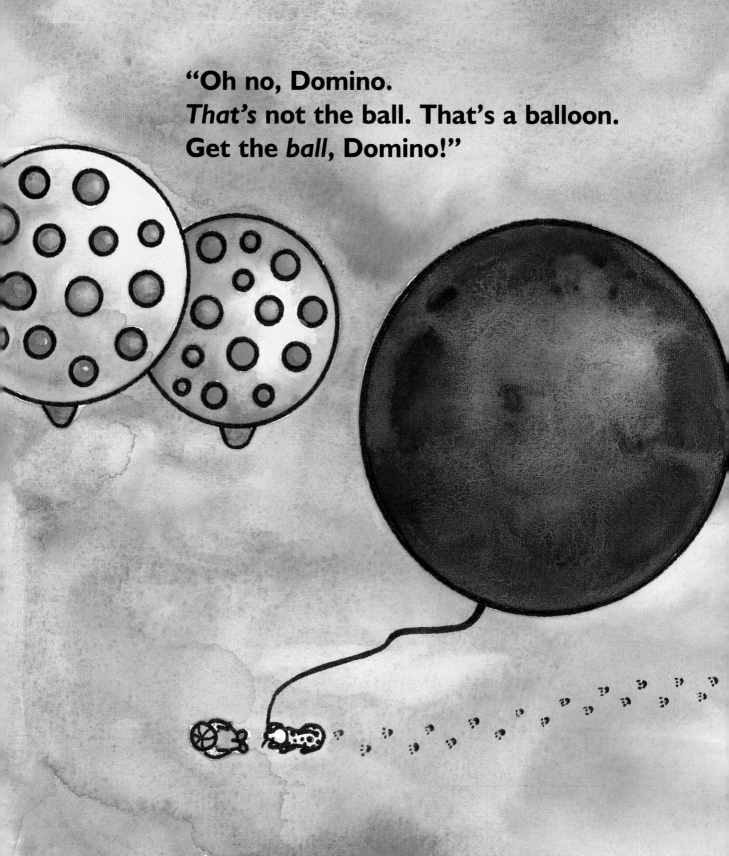

"Oh no, Domino.
That's not the ball. That's a balloon.
Get the *ball*, Domino!"

"BARK!"

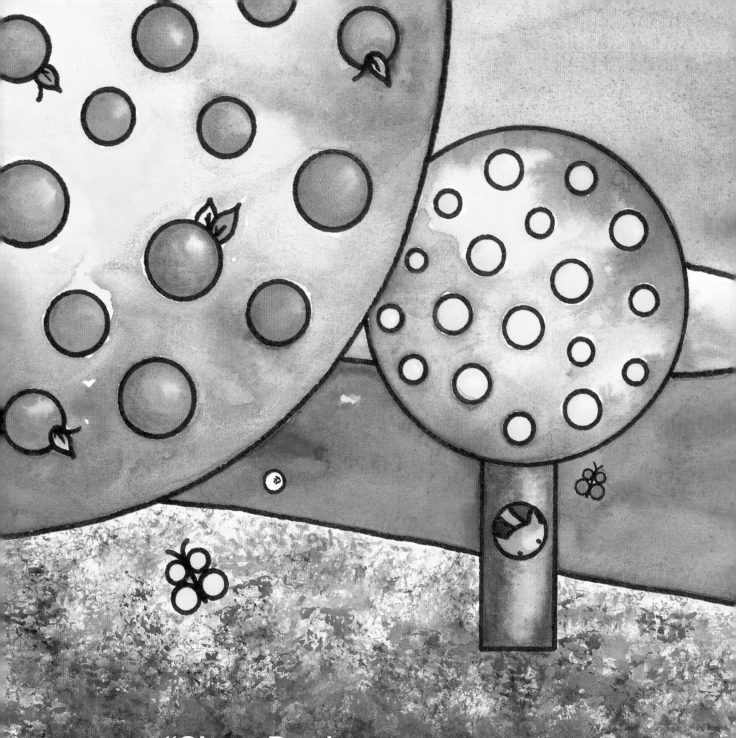

"Oh no, Domino.
That's not the ball. That's a bubble.
Get the *ball*, Domino!"

"Oh no, Domino.
That's not the ball. That's your spot.
Get the *ball*, Domino!"

"Oh no, Domino!
That's *definitely* not the ball! That's the sun!
It's okay, Domino. We'll find it tomorrow."

"Meow."